alm, Jerry
ones an

THADDEUS JONES and THE DRAGON

Story and Pictures by Jerry Hjelm

published by

ODDO PUBLISHING
Fayetteville, Georgia
Symbol for exciting book ideas

Dedicated to my MOTHER

managing editor

Genevieve Oddo

Advisers

Anita Bullard
Assistant Professor of English
Oswego State University College, New York

Ruth Foy
Library Coordinator
Baldwin-Whitehall Public Schools
Pittsburgh, Pennsylvania

Jean Henschel
President
Educational Research and Consultation Services
Tucson, Arizona

Norbert C. Lopez
Superintendent of Schools
Espanola, New Mexico

Nina Martin
Coordinator, ESEA Title II
Montgomery, Alabama

Rae Oetting
Member, Outdoor Writers of America

Mel Schumacher
Coordinator, General Curriculum
Monterey County Office of Education, California

Alvin M. Westcott
Associate Professor of Elementary Education
Oswego State University College, New York

Reading Consultant
William E. Jones
Director of Education
D'Youville College
Buffalo, New York

Library of Congress Catalog Card Number 68-56830.
Printed in the United States of America. Library Binding
Third Printing 1970

CHAPTER I

In a far-off land, there was once a great and prosperous kingdom, as peaceful and contented as one could dream. This was a happy realm, where a knight with a sword was a man—and a man might even find a stray dragon here and there. It was, as the people of that country sometimes said, a picture-book land, for the houses—humble or great—were surrounded by gardens, and through everything there wound a swift blue river.

Deep in the heart of the kingdom, at the top of a steep hill high above the green checkered countryside, sat a great castle, whose turrets and towers stretched through the clouds to the sky. This was the home of the King and Queen, and their young daughter, a princess. Other people lived here, too: soldiers and servants, wizards and wise men, great teachers and famous warriors, and a young man named Thaddeus Jones. And so, this is the story of the boy, Thaddeus, and a dragon named Dudley—and how the boy and the dragon became friends—and how Dudley learned that to be different from others is no crime.

Thad Jones was a dreamer. He dreamed and dreamed of fine things—of how he would some day be a famous knight and own a gold palace, or at least a country home, of the dozens of horses he would have, and of being a hero. But Thad was not a soldier, nor even a palace guard. Many years earlier the King, disguised as a peddler, had ridden his horse through the little town in which Thad and his father, a poor farmer, lived. He had often visited his subjects so disguised, but this time the horse stumbled on a rock and fell, and the King had hurt his leg. Thad's father had helped the King to his own small house, treated his injured leg and given him food to eat. Before returning to his castle, the King had revealed who he was.

"I promise," he told them, "that neither you nor your son shall ever want for any good thing." Several years later, Thad's father died, and the King brought the boy to his palace to live.

But the Queen was not so fond of Thad. She was a strong-willed but sometimes wrong-headed woman who knew what she wanted! She admired young men of courage and action. Day dreamers such as Thaddeus would never amount to anything, she insisted — and so, Thad kept out of her sight as well and as often as he could.

It was late spring and the last trace of snow had vanished from the shaded hillside. Yellow and white flowers dotted the land below and on this early, golden morning, a light breeze brushed the green-turning trees of the forest. On the hilltop, in the castle, the King and Queen were discussing important matters.

"While you're about it," Her Majesty was declaring in a voice like a battle trumpet, "find some way to get our daughter married."

"But—" said the King.

"No, don't talk back to me," she answered. "Do you think we can support her all the rest of our old age? Here she is, hard on nineteen and there isn't a likely prince in the countryside. You must do something about it!"

The King frowned and rubbed his forehead. Yes, something must be done; that was clear. It was not that the princess wasn't beautiful—no, that was not the problem. But she could not be allowed to marry just any butcher or baker, and the only eligible prince of nearly her age lived in a kingdom hundreds of miles to the south, and he would soon marry another.

Well, this was a fine problem indeed, but what the King and Queen did not know was that a far larger and more serious problem would soon arise. Thad, you see, was in love with the princess. And while the princess was, perhaps, not actually in love with him, she was very fond of him—perhaps more fond than a princess should be of an ordinary citizen with no royal blood. Though this made little difference to her, she knew well of her mother's dislike for Thad, and this she dared not forget.

So, while the King and Queen were discussing the matter of the marriage of the princess, Thad was speaking to her about another matter.

There was to be a ball that evening in the castle garden. Would she, he wondered, like to go with him?

"I'm sorry, Thad," she was saying unhappily, "but I can't go with you tonight. I must help Mother polish her jewelry." Thad recognized this as an excuse, and not a very good one.

"How about tomorrow night then?" he asked.

"I'm afraid I'll be busy then too—and Mother said—"

"Yes, I know," said Thad sadly, and turned to leave. He couldn't recall when he had felt so lonely.

Near the end of the main palace hall, Thad heard someone call his name and looked around to see Willard, one of the King's servants, running toward him.

"Thad, the castle supply of Instant Magic is almost gone. The King would like you to stop in to see Meteoras, the Magician, and get a couple of gallons. He has a new batch he's anxious to test."

"All right, Willard. Thanks," replied Thad. "I have nothing else to do."

CHAPTER II

Instant Magic? It was used to treat the unhappy subjects of the King, of whom there were a few. While no one was forced to take it against his will — except for robbers or outlaws who had no choice in the matter — it was a wondrous liquid which produced astonishing and often permanent changes in the people to whom it was given to drink. Those who had hated no longer hated. The greedy and dishonest

became unselfish and loyal. It was a remarkable discovery and something without which the kingdom would have been a much more difficult place to manage.

"Perhaps," thought Thad, as he made his way along the path through the woods which led to the magician's workshop, "perhaps the Queen should drink some."

Presently he arrived at the base of the high stone tower in which Meteoras did his magic work. The door was open so he stepped inside and began climbing the eight-hundred and thirty-seven steps that spiralled round and round to the room at the top where he mixed his mysterious potions.

The magician was a little crazy, as great men sometimes are, but Thad liked him and was his friend. He wondered why the old man was content to practice his magic in such a small kingdom when he could have been famous throughout the neighboring countries if he had chosen. He was surely as talented a sorcerer as the great Merlin, and perhaps more so.

As he climbed the stairs it grew dark; he feared that soon he would not be able to see at all. Up, up and up he went, growing breathless with effort, until at last he pulled a tired leg over the top step. Thad paused to catch his breath and saw that the heavy oak doors to the workshop were closed and no doubt locked. He knocked. There wasn't a sound.

This double-page illustration has been judged the best color cartoo of the year in the Professional Division of the annual competitio sponsored by the Minneapolis Art Instruction Schools, for 1964.

He reached to knock a second time, but the doors had begun to move — they shivered and slithered and looked unreal. They were alive! Then, in a sudden gust of wind, they disappeared like a bursted soap bubble, and Thad stood looking through an open archway into the haze-filled, dark and cluttered room where Meteoras was seated in the

far corner, measuring powders onto a scale. To the left of where Thad was standing, a stone fireplace covered the entire wall, and over the bright blaze there hung a huge copper cauldron, filled with a green, bubbling liquid. "Come in, Thaddeus, my friend," said the old man, without turning in his chair.

The magician was unbelievably tall and thin, with thick white hair on the back of his head and the longest nose in the kingdom. He wore a pointed blue cap on which were painted strange shapes and designs which Thad did not understand. Over his bony body was draped a dark blue cape of the kind worn by all court magicians. A black crow sat on his shoulder, muttering to itself.

"Are you making some of the new Instant Magic, Me-te-or-as?" Thad loved the magician's name and never had trouble pronouncing it properly. He stepped cautiously through the place where the door had been.

"Yes, my lad. The new improved formula I guarantee to produce more incredible and more complete results than have ever been known," he chuckled happily, pouring the powder he had just measured into a round, tall-necked bottle.

"I must recite the words once more to be certain that I have overlooked nothing," he said as he unrolled a sheet of ancient, patched parchment with his long wrinkled fingers.

" 'Whiskers from a spotted cat,
Wing of bat, front tooth of rat;
Feather from a cobbler's hat,
With magic words stirred in the vat.'

"And —" he paused. "Licorice — for flavor. Have some." He held out a brown paper sack to Thad.

"Take the whole sack, my boy."

Thad thanked the old man and tucked the sack inside his shirt.

"And now," declared the magician in a shaky voice, "I will bring the mixture to a boil and add the magic-possessing powders. I must warn you to stand well back from the cauldron and hold your ears, for anything can and may happen!" Holding the bottle of powders in his hand, Meteoras

stepped quickly to the fireplace and dropped them, bottle and all, into the smouldering, bubbling vat — then scrambled, almost tripping on his cumbersome robe, to the opposite end of the room where he crouched behind a table, next to Thad. Shrieking, the crow flew to the rafters, high overhead.

"Throw yourself on the floor!" shouted the magician. "It's going to explode!"

No sooner had the old man and the boy fallen to the floor, than a blinding flash of blue light filled the room and a shattering explosion sent bottles and boxes flying in all directions. They were sheltered by the table, but shaken all the same.

When the dust had settled, the magician turned to Thad and clasped him by the shoulders.

"A magnificent reaction!" he grinned. "We will make wizardry history!"

CHAPTER III

Now, it need not be said that the kingdom was sometimes not so peaceful and contented as the citizens of the land could dream, for in that day dragons roamed the face of the earth — fire breathing dragons that sought trouble and desired to make people as unhappy as they were themselves.

About twelve miles to the west of the kingdom an enormous, dark and damp cave opened into the side of a rocky hill, and in the cave there lived the unhappiest of all the dragons. This unfortunate beast's name was Dudley. He was eighteen feet tall when he stood up, and covered from head to pointed tail with green and blue scales.

Why was Dudley so unhappy? First, because he could not breathe fire, as could the other dragons. Second, because he was educated, as were none of the other dragons. Being educated, he understood — as the others did not — the hatred and fear with which men regarded him and his fellow-dragons. And so, because of his misery, Dudley was truly the most feared of all the dragons, for he was the most troublesome.

For two days, Dudley's cave had been empty. This could mean only one thing — trouble.

At this moment Dudley was approaching the edge of the village. He had spent a day in the forest, teaching himself how to smoke the big, black cigars which he had stolen from a travelling peddler who had passed through town the week before. To his delight, he had discovered that he could imitate, by

blowing the smoke from several cigars at once through his nose, the same terrible effects that the fire-breathing dragons produced.

"So this is how it feels to breathe fire," muttered Dudley.

"I can think of better ways to make a living."

Pulling his tail up behind his back, he sat down under a tree by a stream to decide from which way to approach the castle. He scratched his scaly back and took a deep puff. Letting out the smoke, he tried to give a dragon-snort at the same time, but managed only to sneeze and cough fitfully.

"I must be careful not to overdo it," he gasped.

He folded his hands over his stomach and rested, trying to think of what mischief he could create at the castle.

"I could pull up the apple trees in the orchard, stuff them in the chimneys and smoke them out — or — I could beat my tail on the ground outside the kitchen window and make all the cakes fall. Nope—baking day was yesterday."

But a sinister idea was forming in the back of his mind. Slowly an evil look crept over his face; his eyes narrowed; he rested his chin on his hand and began to puff furiously on the five cigars in his mouth. He had an absolutely enormous idea — almost frightening, it was so daring, and so simple. He would be King!

CHAPTER IV

It was now afternoon, and seated at a table in the palace garden, His Majesty, the King, and Chester, the Court Jester, were playing checkers. By the smile on his face, you could tell that at the moment the King was winning. Chester stared at the board, while the King was thinking that it would soon be time to begin making the garden ready for to-night's ball.

At that moment, one of the guards burst through the gate carrying a scrap of paper in his hand and excitedly shouting:

"Your Majesty! The Princess! A dragon has carried her away!"

The King jumped to his feet, upsetting the table and scattering checkers on the ground.

DEAR KING, I HAVE CAPTURED YOUR DAUGHTER. IF YOU WANT TO SEE HER AGAIN, YOU MUST FORFEIT YOUR CROWN—AND YOUR CASTLE—TO ME (SIGNED) Dudley

"What? How rude! A plague on that dragon! A thousand plagues! Call the guards! Fetch my sword! Bring me some tea!"

Chester kneeled to pick up the fallen checkers as the King, frowning, read the note which the guard had handed him.

"By my mother's beard!" shouted the King, gathering his robes around him and walking swiftly toward the garden gate. "The dragon will pay for this!"

He entered the castle, followed by Chester and the guard, and headed directly for the throne room.

"What shall we do? What shall we do?" he repeated.

He seated himself wearily on the throne and put his head in his hands.

Uneasily, Chester and the guard stood some distance away, waiting to see what course of action he would take. Several minutes passed as the King, lost in troubled thought, tried to think of a plan. Yes — perhaps that would work — no. But if he were to —

His frown became a smile. He clapped his hands on his knees and shouted:

"I have it! We'll issue a proclamation. Anyone catching the dragon gets half the kingdom and my daughter's hand in marriage, to boot!"

A brilliant idea! For the dragon's captor would be knighted, thus making him eligible to marry the princess — and the kingdom would be rid forever of the terrible dragon.

Hardly an hour had passed before several of the proclamations had been printed and posted in the castle. In the main hall, a crowd of soldiers and guards were gathered before one of them to read the message. Among the group was Thad.

The others were all talking excitedly at once:

"Look! A message from the King."

"There must be real trouble. His Majesty never issues a proclamation without good reason."

"But no one in the palace would tackle that dragon even with the sharpest sword in the kingdom."

"A crime, that's what it is."

"What about us? What will happen if the dragon takes possession of the castle?"

THE KING

But Thad said nothing. He had read the King's message and was now walking quietly away from the group toward the room on the floor above where he slept. On the wall in the room hung a long, pointed steel sword in a beautifully decorated sheath of brass. Next to it hung a wide leather belt with a round gold buckle.

Thad carried the sword and the belt down from their place on the wall and, strapping them around his waist, tested the edge of the sword by rubbing his thumb lightly against it. Yes, it was sharp! Thad spun around toward the door and walked out of the room. He and Dudley would soon meet!

CHAPTER V

The dragon, meanwhile, had taken the captured princess to his cave-home and tied her to a chair. Lighting the fourth of the five cigars in his mouth, he coughed violently, turned to her and said:

"Why so gloomy, Princess? Don't like it here, eh?"

He finished lighting the fifth cigar and blew a thick cloud of grey smoke into the room.

"Well, I probably won't have to keep you here much longer. The King must have gotten my letter by now."

The Princess angrily strained and pulled at the ropes holding her to the chair.

"Father will never agree to your terms! He'll fight back!

Why do you suppose you failed in your other attempts to take over the castle?"

Dudley folded his arms behind his head and leaned back.

"Yes, Princess, but this is different. Until now, I failed to include you in my plans. I predict that within the next twenty-four hours I will be the new ruler. King Dudley the First! The other dragons will be required by law to respect me!"

At this happy thought, he jumped to his feet, excitedly puffing smoke and thumping his tail on the floor.

"The castle will be mine! I'll have a hundred slaves to do nothing but make cigars! I'll sleep on featherbeds! Every man in the country will be my servant! They'll work twelve hours a day! They'll pay a tax on the food they eat! I'll charge a dollar an hour for the privilege to breathe!"

Dudley glanced out the window. Someone was coming; a short distance up the road that curved past the entrance to the cave he saw what appeared to be a young man, wearing the clothes of a servant to the King and carrying a sword at his waist.

"So they've sent a boy to do a man's job," thought Dudley.

Thad had been walking since early morning, and as it was now well past noon, the sun was hot and he was growing tired. Ahead of him, he saw the heavy wooden door which opened into Dudley's cave. This was new country to him and he could not know that he was now standing right in front of the place for which he was looking!

"Somebody must live here," he thought to himself. "Maybe they know where the dragon lives. It won't hurt to ask." He knocked.

"I hope someone is home," he said aloud.

"Come in," answered Dudley, as he swung open the door, grabbed Thad by the collar and pulled him roughly inside. Thad reached frantically for his sword, but Dudley had already yanked it from the sheath and thrown it into the corner, out of reach. It was hopeless to struggle, Thad knew. The dragon was a good deal stronger than he. Quickly, Dudley tied the boy's hands behind his back and placed him next to the window.

"You won't untie those knots, son," he said; "but now, pardon me while I dash off another note to the Princess' father. He will want to know about this."

Dudley reached up to a shelf high on the wall, produced a pad of paper, a quill pen and a bottle of ink, then heaved himself onto a low stool next to a small table by the window. He dipped the quill in the ink and began to scratch out the letter. He finished it quickly and tore it from the pad, and reaching up to the shelf again, he brought down—this time—a small cage.

Dudley opened the door of the cage and lifted out a little grey carrier pigeon. He rolled the note around its leg and tied it in place, then raised open the window and released the bird.

"To the King, Homer," he shouted; "and fly your fastest!"

Then he slammed the window shut, settled himself on the floor next to it, and fell asleep.

CHAPTER VI

In the castle, the King and Chester were half-heartedly playing another game of checkers, waiting for news of Thad and the Princess.

"Methinks we should give up the game, Chester," His Majesty said wearily. "Seems as though bad news always comes while we're playing."

The Jester looked up from the board just in time to see the dragon's little bird fly through the window into the room.

"Verily, sir! I believe you're right. I see some on the way."

The pigeon fluttered to the table.

"Another message from the dragon?"

"I'm afraid so."

Gently the King picked up the bird and took the note from its leg. As he read it his face became angry, then hopelessly sad. Slowly he removed the crown from his head and placed it in the center of the checkerboard, then stood and walked toward the door.

"Your Majesty! Where are you going?" cried the jester.

"I'm going to sign a warrant giving over the castle and crown to the dragon, pack my bags and leave."

"But—"

"Read the note." He tossed it at the Jester.

"Dear King," Dudley had written, "I have just captured Thaddeus Jones. I know that you would like to see him again, and also your daughter. Please leave the key to the castle in the hollow willow tree by the foot-bridge on the road that leaves town. Then follow the road out of town.

Dudley"

The King paused in the doorway and said, "You'll probably want to leave, too, before he arrives. Warn everyone in the castle."

CHAPTER VII

Dudley awakened from his short nap, stretched and yawned an enormous, shuddering yawn. He took five fresh cigars from the box on the table and slowly lighted each one, blowing huge clouds of smoke that made Thad's eyes water and caused the Princess to sneeze violently.

"Well," the dragon chuckled, "I'd almost forgotten you chaps were here. How about a game of checkers?"

"You could open a window," replied Thad.

Dudley turned to Thad and blew a cloud of smoke in his face.

Thad attempted to turn away from the dragon. But what was it he felt inside his shirt? He had eaten the licorice jelly beans, but Metoras had given him something else—a small

bottle of Instant Magic for his own personal use. It had given Thad an idea. Dudley turned his head for a moment and Thad leaned forward as far as he could. The bottle fell to the floor and rolled toward the dragon. Dudley grabbed it, examined it closely and pulled the cork. The liquid inside began to bubble. Thad's mind was racing now.

"Don't drink that, Dragon!" he shouted. "It tastes like fish oil and makes fire in your stomach. You'll be breathing smoke for days!"

Suspiciously, Dudley glared at Thad. Then he smiled, brought the bottle to his lips and drank it all in one gulp. Thad scarcely dared to breathe.

"Not bad." The dragon smacked his lips and placed the empty bottle on the table, patted his stomach and settled back against the wall, feeling rather pleased. Soon, now, the King

would be leaving the palace for good. In another two or three hours, he—Dudley—would seat himself on the throne, snap his fingers and an attendant would polish his scales. Later, he would order the royal sorcerer to create gallons and gallons of the potion which would permit him to breathe, as the other dragons did, real fire. Of course, all this was wrong, but what did he care? What, indeed? But after all, he must admit it was wrong. Well, so what? He might permit the ex-king to remain as an advisor or foreign minister. He had been a good king.

Dudley drew a trembling hand across his forehead. Why did he feel so strange? Was he becoming ill? Never in his life had he been sick. Dragons did not get sick! But with a shudder, he suddenly howled and leaped to his feet, his head spinning and eyes bulging. He began to sway this way

and that, forward and backward, from side to side. Slowly at first, then faster, faster and still faster he moved, the sickening wave of dizziness growing inside him. He shook wildly and wailed so loudly that the windows rattled. Thaddeus and the princess stared, not daring to believe what they saw. A ghostly greenish light had seemed to surround Dudley, and as it grew dimmer, the dragon's eyes slowly closed and his shaking became less violent. Soon he was calm and now stood almost perfectly still, his hands hanging lifelessly at his side. Then, with an enormous groan, he collapsed into a quivering heap on the floor.

CHAPTER VIII

His Majesty, the King, was dragging his feet. He looked nothing like the great and famous ruler who had never lost a battle. "Oh woe," he moaned as he walked. "Woe, woe, woe. A plague on that dragon. A thousand times ten thousand plagues on that miserable beast."

The rough road which led north from town followed the edge of the forest for a distance of about a half-mile before it dipped and curved toward the west, crossing the river as it left the forest. To the eyes of the King, it disappeared from view entirely a short way ahead, where it turned. "Woe, woe, woe," repeated the King. "Why oh why didn't I—"

But what was that sound? He stopped, listening. There was a great commotion ahead, but what caused it he could not tell, for the trees were dense, and he could see the road only a few feet further. As he listened, the noise grew louder—or was it coming closer? Were some of the wild animals of the forest having a fight to the death? But no. It seemed to be a celebration of some sort. Now someone was singing. They should be coming around the bend in a moment. The King would let them pass before continuing on his way to the river.

He could just see them now, and at the same moment, the tall member of the group—for there were three of them—spotted him and bellowed.

"The King! The old boy himself! We were just talking about you!" It was the dragon!

The King's mouth hung open. He was dreaming, surely. No doubt he had fallen asleep by the tree under which he had stopped to rest several minutes earlier. But this was no dream.

"What is this all about?" he demanded. Dudley put his hand on the King's shoulder.

"Your Majesty," he began, "I'm a changed dragon. I don't know what ever possessed me. I was a fool! Whoever heard of a dragon ruling a kingdom? I'd always dreamed of owning a castle someday. As a youth, I often built imaginary castles in the air — wild dreams they were — of being famous far and wide as the only creature in dragondom with an education."

The shaken King sat on a rock, his hands on his knees, his face tired.

Dudley continued: "I was befriended years ago by a young student who wanted to become a teacher. He agreed to teach me all that he knew—which was a great deal—and then display me to all the world as his own student. But the more I learned, the more unhappy I became. The unhappier I became, the more cruel and beastly I grew. Finally the young man was so afraid of me that he refused to see me any longer. But I didn't care; all that mattered was that I somehow learn to breathe fire. Then I discovered these foul-tasting cigars."

"And why," asked the King, "have you changed?"

"I drank a bottle of your wizard's magical potion," he explained, "and it helped me to think clearly for the first time. I realized that being different doesn't matter! A smokeless dragon should be as proud of his shiny scales and long tail as a dragon with smoke—and feel better, besides."

The King grinned. "I'll double his wages," he declared. "No. I'll triple them."

In the happy days that followed, the people of the town celebrated joyously, for there was much to celebrate. The kingdom was saved! Meteoras, the Magician, was acclaimed throughout the land as the finest wizard in the world. The dragon, happy at last, had been given a home in the palace and was appointed, because of his education, special advisor on dragon problems to His Majesty, the King. Thaddeus had found favor in the eyes of the Queen. He was a man; she knew this now, beyond all doubt. Peace and contentment reigned once more.

And did Thaddeus Jones and the Princess one day marry and live happily ever after?

Well, what do you suppose?

author
and
illustrator

Jerry Hjelm was born in Joliet, Illinois in 1936. Since the age of two he has made his home in St. Paul, Minnesota.

As he states, "I began drawing at about 2:15 P.M., July 12, 1942, and haven't stopped since."

Jerry Hjelm attended the Minneapolis School of Art and has continued his training through home-study courses. He is currently employed in the Art Department of a nationally known advertising firm.

In his creation of art for all age groups and organizations, he came to understand youngsters, their likes and dislikes, which prompted him to use his writing ability in "THADDEUS JONES AND THE DRAGON."

His major hobbies are Music (records and tape-making), Photography, and Painting.